An I Can Read Book™

STUART LITTLE™

Stuart at the Fun House

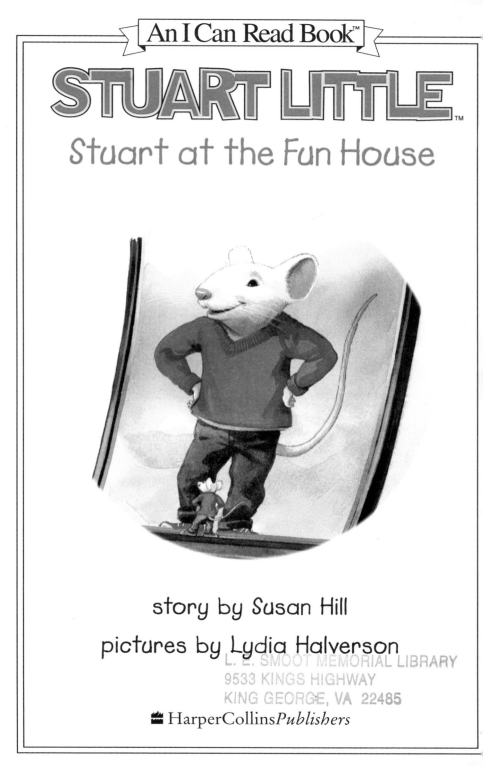

story by Susan Hill

pictures by Lydia Halverson

HarperCollins*Publishers*

Stuart at the Fun House
Story by Susan Hill
Text and illustrations copyright © 2001 by
Columbia Pictures Industries, Inc. All rights reserved.
Printed in the U.S.A. All rights reserved.
www.harperchildrens.com

Library of Congress Cataloging-in-Publication Data
Hill, Susan.
    Stuart at the fun house / by Susan Hill ; pictures by Lydia Halverson.
        p.   cm. — (An I can read book)
    Summary: When Stuart Little and his brother, George, go to the amusement park, George
keeps suggesting rides and games that are too big for Stuart, but the hall of mirrors helps put
things into perspective.
    ISBN 0-06-029539-2 — ISBN 0-06-029635-6 (lib. bdg.) — ISBN 0-06-444304-3 (pbk.)
    [1. Size—Fiction. 2. Amusement parks—Fiction. 3. Brothers—Fiction. 4. Mice—Fiction.]
I. Halverson, Lydia, ill. II. Title. III. Series.
PZ7.H5574 Sr 2001   00-050557
[E]—dc21   CIP
                                                                                              AC

1   2   3   4   5   6   7   8   9   10
❖
First Edition

Stuart at the Fun House

One day
Stuart Little and his brother, George,
went to an amusement park.

"Look at all the rides!"
George said.

"Look at all the food!"
Stuart said.

"This is great!" said George.

"I always wanted a brother

to go to the amusement park with."

"I'm your man!" Stuart said.

"What do you want to do first,
Stuart?" asked George.

"I want to do what you want to do,"
said Stuart.

"Look, there's the strong man game!"
said George.

"Well, I don't think . . . ,"
Stuart started to say.

But George had already run ahead.
Stuart followed.

George picked up the hammer
and swung it hard.
"We have a winner!"
the man shouted.

"Your turn, Stuart," George said.

Stuart looked at the hammer.

"Do you have any other sizes?"

Stuart asked the man.

"One size fits all," the man said.

11

"I guess you need a strong brother
to play this game, George,"
Stuart said.

"That's okay, Stuart.

Let's try the pony ride,"

said George.

13

George and Stuart got on their ponies.

All the ponies began to walk

faster and faster.

14

Stuart's pony didn't move.

"Giddyap!" shouted Stuart.

The pony lady laughed.

"You're not heavy enough to ride!

The pony doesn't know

you're on his back," she said.

Stuart waited for George to finish.

"I guess you need a big brother

for this ride, George,"

said Stuart.

"That's okay, Stuart,"

George said.

"Let's try the roller coaster!"

Stuart and George stood in line

for the ride.

The cars on the track looped

up and down and

around and around.

People got on and off.

"Hurray! We're finally at the front of the line," George said.

"Next!" shouted the man.

"That's us," said Stuart.

"Sorry, kid," the man said to Stuart.
He pointed at a sign.
"You must be this high
to ride the roller coaster."

"I guess you need a tall brother
for this ride," said Stuart.
"You go on without me."
Stuart waited on the ground
and watched George.

"Now what, Stuart?"

asked George when the ride was over.

"How about the fun house?"

"Okay," said Stuart.

"The fun house sounds . . . fun."

Stuart and George paid for their tickets
and went inside the fun house.

A sign said:

ENTERING THE HALL OF MIRRORS.

They stepped inside.

The mirrors made them look wobbly.

The mirrors made them look wiggly.

Suddenly, they stopped
and stared.

"Look, George! I'm big now!"
Stuart said.

"And I'm small!" George said.

Big Stuart looked at little George.

Little George looked at big Stuart.

"I'm sorry I kept picking rides and
games for regular-size people,"
the tiny George said.

"That's okay," the tall Stuart said.

They stepped away from the mirrors.
"Sometimes I forget
you're not stronger, or bigger, or taller.
You're my little brother, and
you're the best brother I ever had,"
George said.

"Thanks, George," Stuart said.

"Now you pick a ride, Stuart!"
said George.

Stuart smiled.